Before Success

Before Success
The Beginning with No Ending

K'BANA BLAQ

4-U-Nique
Publishing
Breaking the Status Quo, One Book at a Time.™

4-U-Nique Publishing
A Series of VLB/VBJ Enterprises, LLC

4-U-Nique Publishing books may be purchased for
educational, business, or sales promotional use. For
information, please email: info@4-U-Nique
Publishing.com

First Edition

Cover Design By: K'BANA BLAQ

Cover Images By: Dexter D. Cohen

Back Cover Model (Face Unseen): J. Ortiz

Library of Congress Cataloging-in-Publication Data

ISBN-13: 978-0692149003

ISBN-10: 0692149007

Table of Contents

Welcome

I see the finish line…or is it really the finish line?

I've never really liked the word, *finish*. It has never sat well with me because the word sounds so final. It gives the feeling that everything is complete and there is not any more work to be done. In life I know that is not true, because there is always more to do.

We will run several races in life that are not about competing or getting to the end. I see life as the opposite. Every time I have to run a new race I look at the starting line and do not worry about the finish line. I know my mission is to get to my destination no matter how tired, frustrated, depressed, or confused I may be. I've learned that God is the one who draws the finish line and it is my job to cross it.

The blessing is in the crossing of the finish line, it is the moment you will know when your test is over. At the point you are just preparing to run another race. I want to thank each and every person who reads this. Thank you for watching, cheering, and helping me run my race.

"All things are possible to those that believe"

~ Mark 9:23

"Breathe and Let Go"

Take a moment to release before your day begins and release any of the stress that you allowed to stay with you from yesterday and *LET THEM GO!*

K'BANA BLAQ

That's O.K.

No matter what comes your way, God has created you to win. I have believed this for as long as I can remember. Winning is what I had to do. I knew the road would be rough but it was something burning inside of me that *HAD* to win. I did not have a small goal, but knew early on that God would direct my path. My path was not the traditional route that every parent would want for their child. I wanted to use my God-given talent.

Who knew that I would want to be a star or live the life of a celebrity? I remember going to church and singing my first solo. Mrs. Price gave me the confidence to sing. I had no idea what to expect, so I grabbed the microphone, closed my eyes and started to sing. I only wanted to make my mother proud. I ignored my nerves and just sang. When I finally opened my eyes I was surprised at what I found. Instead of a disappointed mother, I found people worshipping God with tears running down their faces. That feeling of joy has been with me every day after that. My mother raised me to know that God was my source and I should always give Him praise and in that moment I could feel God move. I am so thankful that God allowed her to be my mother.

Standing in front of a welcoming church crowd and being accepted would soon fade. As I grew older, I began to see people look at me differently. As I matured into a young boy the bullying began. Who knew that kids could be so cruel to someone who did not look or act like them? I was on my way to learning a valuable lesson. My love for singing slowly faded the more I was bullied for it. I soon switched to dancing, but not the typical dances that kids my age were doing. I wanted to dance like the Alvin Ailey Dancers and the beautiful Debbie Allen. Dancing was a way to be creative without having to use my voice. Having a high pitch voice and feminine mannerisms was not welcomed. I ended up in a lot of fights and labeled an outcast. I could always depend upon my talent to save me from being a *COMPLETE* outcast.

As a kid, I loved watching *The Wiz* and imagined myself as Dorothy. The love I had for singing eventually led me down a path that would introduce me to my friend Vivian. Vivian and I both loved to dance to Janet Jackson's music. After I decided to attend dance school, God interrupted my plan. A beautiful spirit named Mrs. Rose offered me a solo in the school chorus and my love for singing immediately returned. Although the love for singing returned my days of struggle, heartache, and questioning were far from over. I entered adulthood with some of the same struggles that plagues my childhood.

Every day I would ask myself, *"why"*?

Why God? Why do I have to? Why won't they help me? Why do I keep caring? These questions were just a few that I agonized with daily on this journey to becoming who I am meant to become. Who exactly is that? So many questions and so many thoughts; One thing I knew for sure was that I had to *BECOME*. Become golden. Become happy. Become whole. Become who God called me to be. The hardest thing for me to do is to be me. It seems like it should be easy, but it is one of the hardest realities I deal with daily. In my search to being me I realized that I needed to love others the way I wanted and needed to be loved. I assumed this would be easy, but I was wrong again. I was giving and spreading all of this love and still not feeling complete. I was not receiving the same amount of love back from others that I had given and still getting hurt. I never realized that loving other people would not be the easy solution. Pouring all of this love into others and I still was not *happy*.

With what do you associate the word happiness.? Is it a chance that everyone has or is it something that just happens? I believe that happiness is a choice. It is a choice that I make throughout each day. This is something that I had to learn and master during my career as well as my personal life. However, choosing happiness did not eliminate the challenges I faced. Life dealt me a hand that I had to master. I mastered the art of choosing my thoughts and moods each moment of my day. When I was not receiving the love I needed I still had to choose a mood that would be effective with the portion of the day I was currently in. Being an artist isn't as great as it seems, many people want access to your skill and talent but do not return the effort that you gave. Is that supposed to be ok?

Now let's get real, while I believe happiness is a choice, I do realize that life itself can be outrageous. With so many twists and turns, many times it feels that the moment I get comfortable thinking that things are perfect, this beautiful thing called life steadily throws curveballs in the form of bills, illness, and betrayal. I have experienced being judged, hated on, mistreated, and overlooked but did not quit! Did I want to? Absolutely!

Instead of quitting I did what most people find uncomfortable got real with myself. I decided to stand in front of the mirror and become the judge and jury of my life by being brutally honest with myself. Every insecurity and negative image I had of myself, every wild dream I ever had, I told to the mirror. I began with my self-image. Growing up I was told that I was too dark, too skinny, and ugly. I was teased for wearing glasses, and I was told that I dressed and acted like a girl. These were a few of the thoughts that consumed my mind every day. After hearing these comments so much I started to believe there were true, but I knew in my heart my self-thoughts had to change in order to improve my level of happiness.

Once I laid out all of the negative thoughts I decided to change every negative word to a positive one. Deciding to face these demeaning thoughts took courage and many years to overcome. I could not continue to live with allowing other people's words and judgments to plant roots in my spirit. It was time for me to dig up the negative roots that where attempting to consume my spirit. Ridding myself of all negative thoughts was the first stop on my new journey.

Each positive word worked to build me back up. Day after day I would revisit the mirror and speak positivity into my life. I realized that I was the only one who could choose the path of my destiny. Only I could shape my life. Once I accepted that God gave me this size, skin color and gifts, it became easier to shake the self-hatred. I began to view my glasses as a part of my art. I decided that my sexuality would not be a topic for public discussion or debate. I decided to let God show me who I am instead of listening to what others said I was.

This journey is far from over. I have learned that everyone is not going to love me the way I love them and *that's O.K.*

"Never Destroy"

You will see destruction but you will not be destroyed!

"Don't Doubt"

Stop doubting your gifts and talents and let them open doors for you. So get out of your own way!!!

"Stay Faithful"

Fear is a lie that you only believe when you don't have Faith!

"Excuses Suck"

Be honest when you are not living up to your potential
PERIOD! Now make it happen - PERIOD!

I Gets High

Ok soooooo...that mirror work was not as easy as I believed it would be. Let's be honest, who wants to stand in front of the mirror and address every negative flaw? Along with the mirror work, I started to motivate myself and find something positive to say as I addressed the flaws. I also began to *GET HIGH.* That's right! I began to get high off of life. Being stuck as a child is one thing but now that I'm grown I know I need to face and resolve every distraction. Every morning I make it my business to thank God for allowing me to see another day and maintaining my talents. I not only pray for myself, but I also pray for the gifts and talents of others who enrich the community.

Now that everyone knows that I get high off of life I have moments where I am high for days. I remember meeting Queen Ester Marrow and being guided by her when I played *The Wiz* at the Downing Gross Cultural Arts Theater. Playing that was a blessing, and the engagement taught me many lessons. Meeting her felt like time stood still. She was so gracious and poised, and poured so much love, wisdom, and courage into me that it truly felt like a legitimate life high.

In that moment, I recognized greatness as it was happening. My soul was lifted for weeks to follow. This woman who I considered a legend and family just added another level of courage to my life. Seeing her walking in her purpose encouraged me to walk in mine even more.

Stepping out on faith and taking chances led me to accept an opportunity to travel to Germany and perform in a Prince tribute concert. Unexpectedly, this experience changed my life. Although music is my love, the people and the environment of Germany had the biggest affect on me. I realized during this experience that I was living beneath my worth. I could see that the world was not just black and white. The world is made of beautiful humans made of flesh and blood. Every person is unique and beautiful. The spirit of love was everywhere. Every person that I encountered was welcoming and caring. Witnessing carefree souls proudly being themselves and stepping outside of my life in the United States opened my eyes to a different world that I had not dreamed of.

Returning to the states made me realize just how much hate and negativity I allowed into my life. I had never realized how much energy I gave to the wrong things. Other people's thoughts, feelings, and emotions were beginning to fall onto me and I needed to release them. I harbored those feelings and did not realize it. I decided I would no longer allow other people's opinions to direct my life.

Being in the music industry makes it challenging to shake off the criticisms of others. I mean I'm putting myself out for the world to judge through my music and shows. How do you find the balance between the voices in your head and the voices in front of you? Which voices do you listen to? The tug of war got on my last nerve. Trying to please the fans, trying to be true to myself, and going home and taking off the mask was all starting to feel suffocating. I wanted to be free. If you cannot be your true self then why exist? The question was heavy on my heart.

I opened my mind and my heart to receive the REAL me. I allowed all fear and anxiety to leave and freed up space in my mind. I kept hearing, "It's ok. Don't be afraid to try" in my head. This statement was on repeat and I did not ignore it. The first step to being completely me, meant I had to share myself with my business partner. Preparing to headline at The Norva may not have been the best time to share with him this side of my life but it was a necessity. He had always been supportive - I was nervous because I finally had begun to receive real support. Telling him and seeing his reaction almost put me into a state of depression, but I survived it. The crazy thing is, he was beyond cool with it and then a light bulb went off in my head. As much as I wanted to feel supported, I knew that everyone would not provide support. God reminded me through my business partner that this was a test to see if I really wanted to be myself and still remain in the music business. He will always send the right people at the right time. I was able to pass this test, by not allowing one person's disappointment stop me from following God's calling.

Although I want people to be happy for me, I knew I had to press on and fulfill my purpose. Getting on stage and doing what I love was therapy. That is why writing *"I Gets High"* was so special to me. I wanted to let go of other people's expectation of me and begin to focus on the highs of life. God has truly opened doors for me to share my talent with the world and I will continue to thank Him.

K'BANA BLAQ

"I Am Made to Win"

It's that simple, so accept it!

"Chosen"

Let your name be an action word!

"Just Believe"

It is one of the hardest things to do but in order to be fully successful; you have to believe in yourself!

K'BANA BLAQ

I Can Be Me

I never believed I would have the courage to speak about this topic. But now I do.

All my life I have wanted to be happy but I also know that happiness is not always free. It is a choice that I have to make every day. I realized that many others and myself allowed the opinions and traditions of others guide our individual journey, when it should be testimonies from our personal journeys. I never wanted to be famous until I realized no one liked me for me. To be honest, I love being creative. Creativity provides freedom without judgment, but the reality is that we will all be judged. I had to accept the truth that my identity was being judged, but I did not understand why. As I self-evaluated, I realized I respect others, I give back to my community, and I am a servant of God. However, I am GAY and that is a problem for many.

Being gay has caused some of the saddest days. I have been bullied, assaulted, misjudged, and overlooked. I have even been labeled an outcast while simultaneously being overlooked by the people close to me. The fear of rejection caused me to ignore dating and the pursuit of true love. Fear is powerful.

I did not want the world to see me as gay. I wanted them to see me as someone trying to do right by others while making the world a better place. I feel the good that I do is overlooked and instead I become the topic of gossip and lies. Instead of focusing on gossip I threw myself into my work and used creativity to help others get ahead. In the beginning, I wanted to help as many people as I could, but along the way I started using my gifts to feel love from other people. In reality, much of the love I was being shown was not real love, but situational love.

I found myself in situations that were unsafe nor healthy. Men would want to fight me because I was gay. Being called a faggot or gay in public was humiliating and hurtful. Men were not the only ones who inflicted such pain; women would befriend me only because I was gay as well. In their minds, it was trendy to have a gay friend around. However, as time passed I would learn that I was not truly their friend but someone who was just fun to have around.

What happened to my daily mirror work? It is still a part of my life, but pulling out the positives gets hard. My feelings were hurt once I realized friends only wanted to hang out because they viewed my sexual orientation as a novelty. Yes, I am gay but that does not lessen my worth of my identity as a human and a black man. I live to help others but mankind no matter how much I help, it seems others can only see that I am gay which seems to give people a false rationale to treat me as if I did something wrong. Rather than accept me as I am, many offer me prayers or express that I am too nice to be gay.

I receive the most negativity from places I would have never expected. While I love them dearly and I do not want them affected by my world, their negativity wears on me. Finally, I became fed up with the disapproval and grew tired of making the effort needed to please others. I was killing myself slowly trying to think of others before myself and I had to stop. I wanted and needed real happiness, but knew real happiness would only come with being free. So I went back to the mirror to have an honest conversation with myself.

I have always been aware that God sends people to you on his timing, and after experiencing the shame, rejection, and hurt I met someone who saw me as a genuine friend. He treated me like a human being and nothing else. His motivation and encouragement gave me the spark to keep pushing. We as humans were created to help one another and that is exactly what he was doing for me. His friendship liberated me to be myself and continue working and dreaming.

I have always prayed at night asking God to take the gay away. I no longer want to be considered a criminal or a walking contagious disease. I am tired of being considered an outcast. I longed for God to remove my burden, and when it did not happen I became angry with God for refusing to free me from this prison. It took time to realize that I was the one who had created this prison. I even had the nerve to ask God, "Why me?" and the reply I received blew my mind.

"My grace is sufficient," was the response I heard. I was initially confused and began to cry. However, eventually I came to the realization that we are not perfect beings nor are we meant to be. Our purpose in this life is to maintain faith and believe that our personal destiny will benefit all of mankind. Because I truly believed that my God was great and mighty, I knew I had to forgive people that rejected, disrespected, and judged me. I repeated to myself, - "be so great that they cannot deny you." I chose to wage war on the Devil and not people.

When it comes to my personal freedom, I now know that there are no excuses. I need to let God guide me, while ignoring the opinions of others. I am finally at a place in life where I can say without any hesitation that I am a single human being who loves God and pushes for happiness and unity for all. Not just gay people, but *ALL* people. Now, I am unafraid to pursue and accept true love in my life. I no longer try to hide from what I deserve, instead I happily receive what we *ALL* deserve. Truth now has a place at my dinner table and I will continue to *BE ME*.

"Laughter Over Pain"

Where there is rain surely there will be sun. You have to remind yourself that you carry your own sunshine!

"Enough"

Sometimes you have to say enough is enough!

"I Love All of Me"

I mean love every bit of yourself and all the things that are not perfect inside and out. And realize there is only one you and without you no one could do what you do!

Let Them Go

Letting go is hard for me because I am loyal. I need to learn to wrangle the power of knowing when it is time to let people and situations go when they are not benefiting my journey toward my destiny. My happiness depends on me grasping this concept. At times, I feel like being blessed as a giver can also be a curse. I give expecting nothing in return, but sometime I begin feeling used. At what point do you stop giving when you feel worn down and used?

Learning to let go was necessary in many areas of my life, both professional and personal. Holding onto situations longer than necessary was tricky. God pulled me in one direction while I was still holding onto things and people who God was telling me to let go of. This routine had me feeling like I was constantly riding an unnecessary roller coaster.

Riding a literal rollercoaster may be fun for a time, but emotional rollercoaster rides are long lasting and you tire of them quickly. I had to ask myself, what was preventing me from achieving my purpose and reaching my destiny? The answer was simple; it was I. The realization of the truth hurt, but it was important for me to face and understand it. I was ready to go to the next level by taking charge of my life, career, and relationships. I began letting go immediately. Somehow, along the way I forgot that I needed to care for myself first in order to effectively assist others. I allowed guilt to override my confidence.

I have always known what The Word of God said, yet I still doubted because of fear. I knew this fear was not coming from God, which sent me on a quest to change immediately. I began observing successful peoples' action. I always assumed that putting myself first was selfish, however when I watched other successful people I noticed that they took care of themselves first. Once their goals and desires were met, they were whole, happy and in position to help others.

It sounds like it was easy for me to switch right? Well, it wasn't easy at all. I spent many nights crying and wondering why success kept eluding me. I knew I was a good person. I always made sure that everyone around me had my help in any way they needed. After many more sleepless nights I realized that I had to stop crying and start being honest. As much as I wanted everyone around me to succeed, I knew I was not placed on earth to be a babysitter. I not only had to start being honest with myself but I also had to be honest with the people around me. Being honest started with me feeling comfortable saying *NO* to some things.

Lord, why did I start using that word? I immediately started to see who was for me and who was against me.

Jealousy, anger, and animosity were just a few traits that began to show. These people began to show themselves as users and not friends. It was difficult for them to be happy for me when I made a decision that they did not agree with. These were not the people I needed accompanying me on my journey so I had to let them go.

Unfortunately, with most of life's battles you will have to face God on your own. I have learned that there will not always be a friend around to pull or push you through a problem. The tests that I have been given have made me stronger and wiser. I know that the tests will continue to come, but I no longer see these tests as a punishment from God. Instead I used these tests as a tool for growth. Letting go of things and people are now a part of my healing process. If God says it is time for me to let it go, *I LET GO.*

"Greatest Pusher"

Adversity is your greatest pusher; it has no respect of persons!

"I Speak for Me"

Don't let fear allow people to take advantage of you. Let people know the advantage of listening to you!

"Mouth Control"

You can murder someone with your mouth if you don't
control your tongue!

"Keep Motivated"

Let your creativity keep you motivated everything you
need lives inside of you!

K'BANA BLAQ

Pour Me Out a Blessing

I used to wake every morning wanting nothing but blessings to fall into my life. Do not get me wrong, who does not like a good blessing? My thought process was flawed about how blessings work. I never realized how selfish my thoughts were, I simply expected blessings to flow because I felt I earned them. I had so many friends that were going through hardships in their lives and I was solely focused on blessings for myself. Every day I took for granted the most important blessing in my life. Simply waking up and taking a breath was a blessing in and out of itself. This was the one thing that I was not thanking God for. I am sure many of us tend to skip this simple task.

For many years I was asking God to bless me, but did not realize that I was already blessed. God had done the ultimate; he woke me up. The moment my eyes open I stop in that moment and say *THANK YOU*.

Coming to the realization that I am already blessed has helped me live differently. I now walk, talk and interact with others different. It is such a relief knowing that God is on my side and has already given me one of his biggest blessings, life. *Stop,* complaining and comparing your life to others because you are unique in this world. *Repeat after me,*

"I am whole. I am free to live, love and be a blessing to others. This is the day that the Lord has made.

I will rejoice and be glad in it. I will enter this day with thanksgiving in my heart. I will enter this day with praise. I will say this is the day that the lord has made I will *REJOICE* for he has made me *GLAD*."

Amen

"Listen then Speak"

Sometimes you just have to shut up and take it in and
then wisdom can come from your mouth!

"Suddenly"

Remember, blessings come suddenly!

"Trust your Gut"

That little voice - don't ignore it - you're not crazy!

But GOD

As I sit

And stare into you

I see me

And realize I love you

Why?

Because I made you

And from the beginning

Every step you take

Has been with me

So know this

Through every storm

You have gone through

Know you were with me

And I will never let you go

So when they ask

How you did it

Just say...

"But GOD

ABOUT THE AUTHOR

K'BANA BLAQ is a creative being who allows his gift to flow in all areas of artistry. He is a singer, model, photographer, designer, CEO and now author. K'BANA is a military brat who has traveled to many countries. His travels provided him with a diverse array of experiences, which serves as his inspiration.

His mother, to whom he lost due to cancer, is his greatest influence. She was a fighter and a warrior during her battle. Her faith in God is what left a lasting impression on K'BANA.

Happiness is a choice, especially in life. We'll have days of complete bliss, but then we'll have days where we just want to give up.

K'BANA's mission is to heal the world through his talents - one person at a time. He wants to make his family proud while instilling that same drive in his niece and showing her how to never give up on her dreams.

"This book is the beginning of self-discovery with no end. Letting life be a fantastic journey instead of a graveyard of potential." - K'BANA BLAQ